Cosmo-
politan

Faber
Stories

Akhil Sharma was born in Delhi in India and emigrated to the USA in 1979. His stories have been published in *The New Yorker* and in *Atlantic Monthly*, and have been included in *The Best American Short Stories* and O. Henry Prize Collections. His first novel, *An Obedient Father*, won the 2001 Hemingway Foundation/PEN Award. He was named one of Granta's 'Best of Young American Novelists' in 2007. His second novel, *Family Life*, won the 2015 Folio Prize and was shortlisted for the International Dublin Literary Award 2016. It was followed by *A Life of Adventure and Delight* in 2017. Sharma is currently a Fellow at the New York Public Library's Dorothy and Lewis B. Cullman Center for Scholars and Writers.

# Akhil Sharma

# Cosmo-
politan

**Faber
Stories**

ff

First published in this single edition in 2019
by Faber & Faber Limited
Bloomsbury House
74–77 Great Russell Street
London WC1B 3DA
First published in *A Life of Adventure and Delight* in 2017

Typeset by Faber & Faber Limited
Printed and bound by CPI Group (UK) Ltd, Croydon, CR0 4YY

The right of Akhil Sharma to be identified as author of this work
has been asserted in accordance with Section 77 of the Copyright,
Designs and Patents Act 1988

A CIP record for this book
is available from the British Library

ISBN 978–0–571–35178–7

A little after ten in the morning Mrs. Shaw walked across Gopal Maurya's lawn to his house. It was Saturday, and Gopal was asleep on the couch. The house was dark. When he first heard the doorbell, the ringing became part of a dream. Only he had been in the house during the four months since his wife had followed his daughter out of his life, and the sound of the bell joined somehow with his dream to make him feel ridiculous. Mrs. Shaw rang the bell again. Gopal woke confused and anxious, the state he was in most mornings. He was wearing only underwear and socks, but his blanket was cold from sweat.

He stood up and hurried to the door. He looked through the peephole. The sky was bright and clear. Mrs. Shaw was standing sideways about a foot from the door, and appeared to be staring out over his lawn at her house. She was short and red haired and wore a pink sweatshirt and gray jogging pants.

"Hold on! Hold on, Mrs. Shaw!" he shouted, and ran back into the living room to search for a pair of

1

pants and a shirt. The light was dim, and he had dif-
ficulty finding them. As he groped under and behind
the couch and looked among the clothes crumpled
on the floor, he worried that Mrs. Shaw would not
wait and was already walking down the steps. He
wondered if he had time to turn on the light to make
his search easier. This was typical of the details that
could baffle him in the morning.

Mrs. Shaw and Gopal had been neighbors for
about two years, but Gopal had met her only three or
four times in passing. From his wife he had learned
that Mrs. Shaw was a guidance counselor at the high
school his daughter had attended. He also learned
that she had been divorced for a decade. Her husband, a successful orthodontist, had left her. Since
then Mrs. Shaw had moved five or six times, though
rarely more than a few miles from where she had
last lived. She had bought the small mustard-colored
house next to Gopal's as part of this restlessness.
Although he did not dislike Mrs. Shaw, Gopal was
irritated by the peeling paint on her house and the
weeds sprouting out of her broken asphalt driveway,

as if by association his house were becoming shabbier. The various cars that left her house late at night made him see her as dissolute. But all this Gopal was willing to forget that morning, in exchange for even a minor friendship.

Gopal found the pants and shirt and tugged them on as he returned to open the door. The light and cold air swept in, reminding him of what he must look like. Gopal was a small man, with delicate high cheekbones and long eyelashes. He had always been proud of his looks and had dressed well. Now he feared that the gray stubble and long hair made him appear bereft.

"Hello, Mr. Maurya," Mrs. Shaw said, looking at him and through him into the darkened house, and then again at him. The sun shone behind her. The sky was blue dissolving into white. "How are you?" she asked gently.

"Oh, Mrs. Shaw," Gopal said, his voice pitted and rough, "some bad things have happened to me." He had not meant to speak so directly. He stepped out of the doorway.

The front door opened into a vestibule, and one had a clear view from there of the living room and the couch where Gopal slept. He switched on the lights. To the right was the kitchen. The round Formica table and the counters were dusty. Mrs. Shaw appeared startled by this detail. After a moment she said, "I heard." She paused and then quickly added, "I am sorry, Mr. Maurya. It must be hard. You must not feel ashamed; it's no fault of yours."

"Please, sit," Gopal said, motioning to a chair next to the kitchen table. He wanted to tangle her in conversation and keep her there for hours. He wanted to tell her how the loneliness had made him fantasize about calling an ambulance so that he could be touched and prodded, or how for a while he had begun loitering at the Indian grocery store like the old men who have not learned English. What a pretty, good woman, he thought.

Mrs. Shaw stood in the center of the room and looked around her. She was slightly overweight, and her nostrils appeared to be perfect circles, but her small white Reebok sneakers made Gopal see her as

4

fleet with youth and innocence. "I've been thinking of coming over. I'm sorry I didn't."

"That's fine, Mrs. Shaw," Gopal said, standing near the phone on the kitchen wall. "What could anyone do? I am glad, though, that you are visiting." He searched for something else to say. To extend their time together, Gopal walked to the refrigerator and asked her if she wanted anything to drink.

"No, thank you," she said.

"Orange juice, apple juice, or grape, pineapple, guava. I also have some tropical punch," he continued, opening the refrigerator door wide, as if to show he was not lying.

"That's all right," Mrs. Shaw said, and they both became quiet. The sunlight pressed through windows that were laminated with dirt. "You must remember, everybody plays a part in these things, not just the one who is left," she said, and then they were silent again. "Do you need anything?"

"No. Thank you." They stared at each other. "Did you come for something?" Gopal asked, although he did not want to imply that he was

5

trying to end the conversation.

"I wanted to borrow your lawn mower."

"Already?" April was just starting, and the dew did not evaporate until midday.

"Spring fever," she said.

Gopal's mind refused to provide a response to this. "Let me get you the mower."

They went to the garage. The warm sun on the back of his neck made Gopal hopeful. He believed that something would soon be said or done to delay Mrs. Shaw's departure, for certainly God could not leave him alone again. The garage smelled of must and gasoline. The lawn mower was in a shadowy corner with an aluminum ladder resting on it. "I haven't used it in a while," Gopal said, placing the ladder on the ground and smiling at Mrs. Shaw beside him. "But it should be fine." As he stood up, he suddenly felt aroused by Mrs. Shaw's large breasts, boy's haircut, and little-girl sneakers. Even her nostrils suggested a frank sexuality. Gopal wanted to put his hands on her waist and pull her toward him. And then he realized that he had.

6

"No. No," Mrs. Shaw said, laughing and putting her palms flat against his chest. "Not now." She pushed him away gently.

Gopal did not try kissing her again, but he was excited. Not now, he thought. He carefully poured gasoline into the lawn mower, wanting to appear calm, as if the two of them had already made some commitment and there was no need for nervousness. He pushed the lawn mower out onto the gravel driveway and jerked the cord to test the engine. Not now, not now, he thought, each time he tugged. He let the engine run for a minute. Mrs. Shaw stood silent beside him. Gopal felt like smiling, but wanted to make everything appear casual. "You can have it for as long as you need," he said.

"Thank you," Mrs. Shaw replied, and smiled. They looked at each other for a moment without saying anything. Then she rolled the lawn mower down the driveway and onto the road. She stopped, turned to look at him, and said, "I'll call."

"Good," Gopal answered, and watched her push the lawn mower down the road and up her driveway into the tin shack that huddled at its end. The driveway was separated from her ranch-style house by ten or fifteen feet of grass, and they were connected by a trampled path. Before she entered her house, Mrs. Shaw turned and looked at him as he stood at the top of his driveway. She smiled and waved.

When he went back into his house, Gopal was too excited to sleep. Before Mrs. Shaw, the only woman he had ever embraced was his wife, and a part of him assumed that it was now only a matter of time before he and Mrs. Shaw fell in love and his life resumed its normalcy. Oh, to live again as he had for nearly thirty years! Gopal thought, with such force that he shocked himself. Unable to sit, unable even to think coherently, he walked around his house.

His daughter's departure had made Gopal sick at heart for two or three weeks, but then she sank so completely from his thoughts that he questioned whether his pain had been hurt pride rather than grief. Gitu had been a graduate student and spent only a few weeks with them each year, so it was understandable that he would not miss her for long. But the swiftness with which the dense absence on the other side of his bed unknotted and evaporated made him wonder whether he had ever loved his wife. It made him think that his wife's abrupt decision never to return from her visit to India was as much his fault as God's. Anita, he thought, must have decided upon seeing Gitu leave that there was no more reason to stay, and that perhaps, after all, it was not too late to start again. Anita had gone to India at the end of November—a month after Gitu got on a Lufthansa flight to go live with her boyfriend in Germany—and a week later, over an echoing phone line, she told him of the guru and her enlightenment.

Perhaps if Gopal had not retired early from AT&T, he could have worked long hours and his wife's and daughter's slipping from his thoughts might have been mistaken for healing. But he had nothing to do. Most of his acquaintances had come by way of his wife, and when she left, Gopal did not call them, both because they had always been more Anita's friends than his and because he felt ashamed, as if his wife's departure revealed his inability to love her. At one point, around Christmas, he went to a dinner party, but he did not enjoy it. He found that he was not curious about other people's lives and did not want to talk about his own.

A month after Anita's departure a letter from her arrived—a blue aerogram, telling of the ashram, and of sweeping the courtyard, and of the daily prayers. Gopal responded immediately, but she never wrote again. His pride prevented him from trying to continue the correspondence, though he read her one letter so many times that he inadvertently memorized the Pune address. His brothers sent a flurry of long missives from India, on paper so thin that it was almost translucent, but his contact with them over the decades had been minimal, and the tragedy pushed them apart instead of pulling them closer.

Gitu sent a picture of herself wearing a yellow-and-blue ski jacket in the Swiss Alps. Gopal wrote her back in a stiff, formal way, and she responded with a breezy postcard to which he replied only after a long wait.

Other than this, Gopal had had little personal contact with the world. He was accustomed to getting up early and going to bed late, but now, since he had no work and no friends, after he spent the morning reading *The New York Times* and *The Home News & Tribune* front to back, Gopal felt adrift through the afternoon and evening. For a few weeks he tried to fill his days by showering and shaving twice daily, brushing his teeth after every snack and meal. But the purposelessness of this made him despair, and he stopped bathing altogether and instead began sleeping more and more, sometimes sixteen hours a day. He slept in the living room, long and narrow with high rectangular windows blocked by trees. At some point, in a burst of self-hate, Gopal moved his clothes from the bedroom closet to a corner of the living room, wanting to avoid comforting himself with any illusions that his life was normal.

But he yearned for his old life, the life of a clean kitchen, of a bedroom, of going out into the sun, and on a half-conscious level that morning Gopal decided to use the excitement of clasping Mrs. Shaw to change himself back to the man he had been. She might be spending time at his house, he thought, so he mopped the kitchen floor, moved back into his bedroom, vacuumed and dusted all the rooms. He spent most of the afternoon doing this, aware always of his humming lawn mower in the background. He had only to focus on it to make his heart race. Every now and then he would stop working and go to his bedroom window, where, from behind the curtains, he would stare at Mrs. Shaw. She had a red bandanna tied around her forehead, and he somehow found this appealing. That night he made himself an elaborate dinner with three dishes and a mango shake. For the first time in months Gopal watched the eleven o'clock news. He had the lights off and his feet up on a low table. Lebanon was being bombed again, and Gopal kept bursting into giggles for no reason. He tried to think of what he would do tomorrow. Gopal knew that he was happy and that to avoid depression he must keep himself busy until Mrs. Shaw called. He suddenly realized that he did not know Mrs. Shaw's first name. He padded into the darkened kitchen and looked at the phone diary. "Helen Shaw" was written in the big, loopy handwriting of his wife. Having his wife help him in this way did not bother him at all, and then he felt ashamed that it didn't.

The next day was Sunday, and Gopal anticipated it cheerfully, for the Sunday *Times* was frequently so thick that he could spend the whole day reading it. But this time he did not read it all the way through. He left the *Book Review* and the other features sections to fill time over the next few days. After eating a large breakfast—the idea of preparing elaborate meals had begun to appeal to him—he went for a haircut. Gopal had not left his house in several days. He rolled down the window of his blue Honda Civic and took the long way, past the lake, to the mall. Instead of going to his usual barber, he went to a hair stylist, where a woman with long nails and large, contented breasts shampooed his hair before cutting it. Then Gopal wandered around the mall, savoring its buttered-popcorn smell and enjoying the sight of the girls with their sometimes odd-colored hair. He went into some of the small shops and looked at clothes, and considered buying a half pound of cocoa amaretto coffee beans, although he had never cared much for coffee. After walking for nearly two hours, Gopal sat on a bench and ate an ice cream cone while reading an article in *Cosmopolitan* about what makes a good lover. He had seen the magazine in CVS and, noting the article mentioned on the cover, had been reminded how easily one can learn anything in America. Because Mrs. Shaw was an American, Gopal thought, he needed to do research into what might be expected of him. Although the article was about what makes a woman a good lover, it offered clues for men as well. Gopal felt confident that given time, Mrs. Shaw would love him. The article made attachment appear effortless. All you had to do was listen closely and speak honestly.

He returned home around five, and Mrs. Shaw

called soon after. "If you want, you can come over now."

"All right," Gopal answered. He was calm. He showered and put on a blue cotton shirt and khaki slacks. When he stepped outside, the sky was turning pink and the air smelled of wet earth. He felt young, as if he had just arrived in America and the huge scale of things had made him a giant as well.

But when he rang Mrs. Shaw's doorbell, Gopal became nervous. He turned around and looked at the white clouds against the enormous sky. He heard footsteps and then the door swishing open and Mrs. Shaw's voice. "You look handsome," she said. Gopal faced her, smiling and uncomfortable. She wore a different sweatshirt, but still had on yesterday's jogging pants. She was barefoot. A yellow light shone behind her.

"Thank you," Gopal said, and then nervously added "Helen," to confirm their new relationship. "You look nice too." She did look pretty to him. Mrs. Shaw stepped aside to let him in. They were in a large room. In the center were two pale couches

15

forming an L, with a television in front of them. Off to the side was a kitchenette—a stove, a refrigerator, and some cabinets over a sink and counter.

Seeing Gopal looking around, Mrs. Shaw said, "There are two bedrooms in the back, and a bathroom. Would you like anything to drink? I have juice, if you want." She walked to the kitchen.

"What are you going to have?" Gopal asked, following her. "If you have something, I'll have something." Then he felt embarrassed. Mrs. Shaw had not dressed up; obviously, "Not now" had been a polite rebuff.

"I was going to have a gin and tonic," she said, opening the refrigerator and standing before it with one hand on her hip.

"I would like that too." Gopal came close to her and with a dart kissed her on the lips. She did not resist, but neither did she respond. Her lips were chapped. Gopal pulled away and let her make the drinks. He had hoped the kiss would tell him something of what to expect.

They sat side by side on a couch and sipped their drinks. A table lamp cast a diffused light over them.

"Thank you for letting me borrow the lawn mower."

"It's nothing." There was a long pause. Gopal could not think of anything to say. *Cosmopolitan* had suggested trying to learn as much as possible about your lover, so he asked, "What's your favorite color?"

"Why?"

"I want to know everything about you."

"That's sweet," Mrs. Shaw said, and patted his hand. Gopal felt embarrassed and looked down. He did not know whether he should have spoken so frankly, but part of his intention had been to flatter her with his interest. "I don't have one," she said. She kept her hand on his.

Gopal suddenly thought that they might make love tonight, and he felt his heart kick. "Tell me all about yourself," he said with a voice full of feeling. "Where were you born?"

"I was born in Jersey City on May fifth, but I won't tell you the year." Gopal tried to grin gamely and memorize the date. A part of him was disturbed that she did not feel comfortable enough with him to reveal her age.

"Did you grow up there?" he asked, taking a sip of the gin and tonic. Gopal drank slowly, because he knew that he could not hold his alcohol. He saw that Mrs. Shaw's toes were painted bright red. Anita had never used nail polish, and Gopal wondered what a woman who would paint her toe-nails might do.

"I moved to Newark when I was three. My parents ran a newspaper-and-candy shop. We sold greeting cards, stamps." Mrs. Shaw had nearly finished her drink. "They opened at eight in the morning and closed at seven thirty at night. Six days a week." When she paused between swallows, she rested the glass on her knee.

Gopal had never known anyone who worked in such a shop, and he became genuinely interested in what she was saying. He remembered his lack of interest at the Christmas party and wondered whether it was the possibility of sex that made him fascinated with Mrs. Shaw's story. "Were you a happy child?" he asked, grinning broadly and then bringing the grin to a quick end, because he did not

18

want to appear ironic. The half glass that Gopal had drunk had already begun to make him feel light-headed and gay.

"Oh, pretty happy," she said, "although I liked to think of myself as serious. I would look at the evening sky and think that no one else had felt what I was feeling." Mrs. Shaw's understanding of her own feelings disconcerted Gopal and made him momentarily think that he wasn't learning anything important, or that she was in some way independent of her past and thus incapable of the sentimental attachments through which he expected her love for him to grow.

*Cosmopolitan* had recommended that both partners reveal themselves, so Gopal decided to tell a story about himself. He did not believe that being honest about himself would actually change him. Rather, he thought the deliberateness of telling the story would rob it of the power to make him vulnerable. He started to say something, but the words twisted in his mouth, and he said, "You know, I don't really drink much." Gopal felt embarrassed

by the non sequitur. He thought he sounded foolish, though he had hoped that the story he would
tell would make him appear sensitive.

"I kind of guessed that from the juices," she said,
smiling. Gopal laughed.

He tried to say what he had wanted to confess
earlier. "I associate drinking with being American,
and I haven't been able to truly Americanize. On
my daughter's nineteenth birthday we took her to
dinner and a movie, but we didn't talk much, and
the dinner finished earlier than we had expected it
would. The restaurant was in a mall, and we had
nothing to do until the movie started, so we wandered around Foodtown." Gopal thought he sounded
pathetic, so he tried to shift the story. "After all my
years in America, I am still astonished by those
huge grocery stores and enjoy walking in them.
But my daughter is an American, so our wandering
around in Foodtown must have been very strange for
her. She doesn't know Hindi, and her parents must
seem very strange." Gopal noticed that his heart was
racing. He wondered if he was sadder than he knew.

"That's sweet," Mrs. Shaw said. The brevity of her response made Gopal nervous.

Mrs. Shaw kissed his cheek. Her lips were dry, Gopal noticed. He turned slightly so that their lips could touch. They kissed again. Mrs. Shaw opened her lips and closed her eyes. They kissed for a long time. When they pulled apart, they continued their conversation calmly, as if they were accustomed to each other. "I didn't go into a big grocery store until I was in college," she said. "We always went to the small shops around us. When I first saw those long aisles, I wondered what happens to the food if no one buys it. I was living then with a man who was seven or eight years older than I, and when I told him, he laughed at me, and I felt so young." She stopped and then added, "I ended up leaving him because he always made me feel young." Her face was only an inch or two from Gopal's. "Now I'd marry someone who could make me feel that way." Gopal felt his romantic feelings drain away at the idea of how many men she had slept with. But the fact that Mrs. Shaw and he had experienced something similar removed some of the loneliness he was feeling, and Mrs. Shaw had large breasts. They began kissing again. Soon they were tussling and groping on the floor.

Her bed was large and low to the ground. Behind it was a window, and although the shade was drawn, the lights of passing cars cast patterns on the opposing wall. Gopal lay next to Mrs. Shaw and watched the shadows change. He felt his head and found that his hair was standing up on either side like horns. The shock of seeing a new naked body, so different in its amplitude from his wife's, had been exciting. A part of him was giddy with this, as if he had checked his bank balance and discovered that he had thousands more than he expected. "You are very beautiful," he said, for *Cosmopolitan* had advised saying this after making love. Mrs. Shaw rolled over and kissed his shoulder.

"No I'm not. I'm kind of fat, and my nose is strange. But thank you," she said. Gopal looked at her and saw that even when her mouth was slack, the lines around it were deep. "You look like you've been rolled around in a dryer," she said, and laughed. Her laughter was sudden and confident. He had not noticed it before, and it made him laugh as well.

They became silent and lay quietly for several minutes, and when Gopal began feeling self-conscious, he said, "Describe the first house you lived in."

Mrs. Shaw sat up. Her stomach bulged, and her breasts drooped. She saw him looking and pulled her knees to her chest. "You're very thoughtful," she said.

Gopal felt flattered. "Oh, it's not thoughtfulness."

"I guess if it weren't for your accent, the questions would sound artificial," she said. Gopal felt his stomach clench. "I lived in a block of small houses that the Army built for returning GIs. They were all drab, and the lawns ran into each other. They were near Newark airport. I liked to sit at my window and watch the planes land."

"Your house was two stories?"

"Yes. And my room was on the second floor. Tell me about yourself."

23

"I am the third of five brothers. We grew up in a small, poor village. I got my first pair of shoes when I left high school." As Gopal was telling her the story, he remembered how he used to make Gitu feel lazy with stories of his childhood, and his voice fell. "Everybody was like us, so I never thought of myself as poor."

They talked this way for half an hour, with Gopal asking most of the questions and trying to discover where Mrs. Shaw was vulnerable and how this vulnerability made him attractive to her. Although she answered his questions candidly, Gopal could not find the unhappy childhood or the trauma of an abandoned wife that might explain the urgency of this moment in bed. "I was planning to leave my husband," she explained casually. "He was crazy. Almost literally. He thought he was going to be a senator or a captain of industry. He wasn't registered to vote. He knew nothing about business. Once, he invested almost everything we had in a hydroponic farm in Southampton. With him I was always scared of being poor. He used to spend two hun-

24

dred dollars a week on lottery tickets, and he would save the old tickets in shoe boxes in the garage." Gopal did not personally know any Indian who was divorced, and he had never been intimate enough with an American to learn what a divorce was like, but he had expected something more painful—tears and recriminations. The details she gave made the story sound practiced, and he began to think that he would never have a hold over Mrs. Shaw.

Around eight Mrs. Shaw said, "I am going to do my bills tonight." Gopal had been wondering whether she wanted him to have dinner with her and spend the night. He would have liked to, but he did not protest.

As she closed the door behind him, Mrs. Shaw said, "The lawn mower's in the back. If you want it." Night had come, and the stars were out. As Gopal pushed the lawn mower down the road, he wished that he loved Mrs. Shaw and that she loved him.

He had left the kitchen light on by mistake, and its glow was comforting. "Come, come, cheer up," he said aloud, pacing in the kitchen. "You have a lover." He tried to smile and grimaced instead. "You can make love as often as you want. Be happy." He started preparing dinner. He fried okra and steam-cooked lentils. He made both rice and bread.

As he ate, Gopal watched a television movie about a woman who had been in a coma for twenty years and suddenly woke up one day; adding to her confusion, she was pregnant. After washing the dishes he finished the article in *Cosmopolitan* that he had begun reading in the mall. The article was the second of two parts, and it mentioned that when leaving after making love for the first time, one should always arrange the next meeting. Gopal had not done this, and he phoned Mrs. Shaw.

He used the phone in the kitchen, and as he waited for her to pick up, he wondered whether he should introduce himself or assume that she would recognize his voice. "Hi, Helen," he blurted out as soon as she said "Hello." "I was just thinking of you and thought I'd call." He felt more nervous now than he had while he was with her.

"That's sweet," she said, with what Gopal thought was tenderness. "How are you?"

"I just had dinner. Did you eat?" He imagined her sitting on the floor between the couches with a pile of receipts before her. She would have a small pencil in her hand.

"I'm not hungry. I normally make myself an omelet for dinner, but I didn't want to tonight. I'm having another drink." Then, self-conscious, she added, "Otherwise I grind my teeth. I started after my divorce and I didn't have health insurance or enough money to go to a dentist." Gopal wanted to ask if she still ground her teeth, but he did not want to imply anything.

"Would you like to have dinner tomorrow? I'll cook." They agreed to meet at six. The conversation continued for a few minutes longer, and when Gopal hung up, he was pleased at how well he had handled things.

While lying in bed, waiting for sleep, Gopal read another article in *Cosmopolitan*, about job pressure's effects on one's sex life. He had enjoyed both articles and was happy with himself for his efforts at understanding Mrs. Shaw. He fell asleep smiling.

The next day, after reading the papers, Gopal went to the library to read the first part of the *Cosmopolitan* article. He ended up reading articles from *Elle*, *Redbook*, *Glamour*, *Mademoiselle*, and *Family Circle*, and one from *Reader's Digest*—"How to Tell If Your Marriage Is on the Rocks." He tried to memorize jokes from the "Laughter Is the Best Medicine" section, so that he would never be at a loss for conversation.

Gopal arrived at home by four and began cooking. Dinner was pleasant, though they ate in the kitchen, which was lit with buzzing fluorescent tubes. Gopal worried that yesterday's lovemaking might have been a fluke. Soon after they finished the meal, however, they were on the couch, struggling with each other's clothing.

Gopal wanted Mrs. Shaw to spend the night, but she refused, saying that she had not slept a full night with anyone since her divorce. At first Gopal was touched by this. They lay on his bed in the dark. The alarm clock on the lampstand said 9:12 in big red figures. "Why?" Gopal asked, rolling over and resting his cheek on her cool shoulder. He wanted to reassure her that he was eager to listen.

"I think I'm a serial monogamist and I don't want to make things too complicated." She twisted a lock of his hair around her middle finger. "It isn't because of you, sweetie. It's with every man."

"Oh," Gopal said, hurt by the idea of other men and disillusioned about her motives. He continued believing, however, that now that they were lovers, the power of his concern would make her love him back. One of the articles he had read that day had suggested that people become dependent in spite of themselves when they are constantly cared for. So he made himself relax and act understanding.

Gopal went to bed an hour after Mrs. Shaw left. Before going to sleep he called her and wished her good night. He began calling her frequently after that, two or three times a day. Over the next few weeks Gopal found himself becoming coy and playful with her. When Mrs. Shaw picked up the phone, he made panting noises, and she laughed at him. She liked his being childlike with her. Sometimes she would point to a spot on his chest, and he would look down, even though he knew nothing was there, so that she could tap his nose. When they made love, she was thoughtful about asking what pleased him, and Gopal learned from this and began asking her the same. They saw each other nearly every day, though sometimes only briefly, for a few minutes in the evening or at night. But Gopal continued to feel nervous around her, as if he were somehow imposing. If she phoned him and invited him over, he was always flattered. As Gopal learned more about Mrs. Shaw, he began thinking she was very smart. She read constantly, primarily history and economics. He was always surprised, therefore, when she became moody and sentimental and talked about how loneliness is incurable. Gopal liked Mrs. Shaw in this mood, because it made him feel needed, but he felt ashamed that he was so insecure. When she did not laugh at a joke, Gopal doubted that she would ever love him. When they were in bed together and he thought she might be looking at him, he kept his stomach sucked in.

This sense of precariousness made Gopal try developing other supports for himself. One morning early in his involvement with Mrs. Shaw he phoned an Indian engineer with whom he had worked on a project about corrosion of copper wires and who had also taken early retirement from AT&T. They had met briefly several times since then and had agreed each time to get together again, but neither had made the effort. Gopal waited until eleven before calling, because he felt that any earlier would make him sound needy. A woman picked up the phone. She told him to wait a minute as she called for Rishi. Gopal felt vaguely deceitful, as if he were trying to pass himself off as just like everyone else, although his wife and child had left him.

"I haven't been doing much," he confessed immediately to Rishi. "I read a lot." When Rishi asked what, Gopal answered "Magazines," with embarrassment. They were silent then. Gopal did not want to ask Rishi immediately if he would like to meet for dinner, so he hunted desperately for a conversational opening. He was sitting in the kitchen. He looked at the sunlight on the newspaper before him and remembered that he could ask Rishi questions. "How are you doing?"

"It isn't like India," Rishi responded. "In India the older you are, the closer you are to the center of attention. Here you have to keep going. Your children are away and you have nothing to do. I would go back, but Ratha doesn't want to. America is much better for women."

Gopal felt a rush of relief that Rishi had spoken so much. "Are you just at home or are you doing something part-time?"

"I am the president of the Indian Cultural Association," Rishi said boastfully.

"That's wonderful," Gopal said, and with a leap added, "I want to get involved in that more, now that I have time."

"We always need help. We are going to have a fair," Rishi said. "It's on the twenty-fourth, next month. We need help coordinating things, arranging food, putting up flyers."

"I can help," Gopal said. They decided that he should come to Rishi's house on Wednesday, two days later.

Gopal was about to hang up when Rishi added, "I heard about your family." Gopal felt as if he had been caught in a lie. "I am sorry," Rishi said.

Gopal was quiet for a moment and then said, "Thank you." He did not know whether he should pretend to be sad. "It takes some getting used to," he said, "but you can go on from nearly anything."

Gopal went to see Rishi that Wednesday, and on Sunday he attended a board meeting to plan for the fair. He told jokes about a nearsighted snake and a water hose, and about a golf instructor and God. One of the men he met there invited him to dinner.

Mrs. Shaw, however, continued to dominate his thoughts. The more they made love, the more absorbed Gopal became in the texture of her nipples in his mouth and the heft of her hips in his hands. He thought of this in the shower, while driving, while stirring his cereal. Two or three times over the next month Gopal picked her up during her lunch hour and they hurried home to make love. They would make love and then talk. Mrs. Shaw had once worked at a dry cleaner, and Gopal found this fascinating. He had met only one person in his life before Mrs. Shaw who had worked in a dry-cleaning business, and that was different, because it was in India, where dry cleaning still had the glamour of advancing technology. Being the lover of someone who had worked in a dry-cleaning business made Gopal feel strange. It made him think that the world was huge beyond comprehension, and to spend his time trying to control his own small world was inefficient. Gopal began thinking that he loved Mrs. Shaw. He started listening to the golden oldies station in the car, so that he could hear what she had heard in her youth.

Mrs. Shaw would ask about his life, and Gopal tried to tell her everything she wanted to know in as much detail as possible. Once, he told her of how he had begun worrying when his daughter was finishing high school that she was going to slip from his life. To show that he loved her, he had arbitrarily forbidden her to ski, claiming that skiing was dangerous. He had hoped that she would find this quaintly immigrant, but she was just angry. At first the words twisted in his mouth, and he spoke to Mrs. Shaw about skiing in general. Only with an effort could he tell her about his fight with Gitu. Mrs. Shaw did not say anything at first. Then she said, "It's all right if you were that way once, as long as you aren't that way now." Listening to her, Gopal suddenly felt angry.

"Why do you talk like this?" he asked.

"What?"

"When you talk about how your breasts fall or how your behind is too wide, I always say that's not true. I always see you with eyes that make you beautiful."

"Because I want the truth," she said, also angry.

Gopal became quiet. Her desire for honesty appeared to refute all his delicate and constant manipulations. Was he actually in love with her, he wondered, or was this love just a way to avoid loneliness? And did it matter that so much of what he did was conscious?

He questioned his love more and more as the day of the Indian festival approached, and Gopal realized that he was delaying asking Mrs. Shaw to come with him. She knew about the fair but had not mentioned her feelings. Gopal told himself that she would feel uncomfortable among so many Indians, but he knew that he hadn't asked her because bringing her would make him feel awkward. For some reason he was nervous that word of Mrs. Shaw might get to his wife and daughter. He was also anxious about what the Indians with whom he had recently become friendly would think. He had met mixed couples at Indian parties before, and they were always treated with the deference usually reserved for cripples. If Mrs. Shaw had been of any sort of marginalized ethnic group—a first-generation immigrant, for instance—then things might have been easier.

The festival was held in the Edison First Aid Squad's square blue-and-white building. A children's dance troupe performed in red dresses so stiff with gold thread that the girls appeared to hobble as they moved about the center of the concrete floor. A balding comedian in oxblood shoes and a white suit performed. Light folding tables along one wall were precariously laden with large pots, pans, and trays of food. Gopal stood in a corner with several men who had retired from AT&T and, slightly drunk, he improvised on jokes he had read in *1,001 Polish Jokes*. The Poles became Sikhs, but the rest remained the same. He was laughing and feeling proud that he could so easily become the center of attention, but he felt lonely at the thought that when the food was served, the men at his side would drift away to join their families and he would be alone. After listening to talk of someone's marriage, he began thinking about Mrs. Shaw. The men were clustered together, and the women conversed separately. They will go home and make love and not talk, Gopal thought.

Then he felt sad and frightened. To make amends for his guilt at not bringing Mrs. Shaw along, he told a bearded man with yellow teeth, "These Sikhs aren't so bad. They are the smartest ones in India, and no one can match a Sikh for courage." Then Gopal felt dazed and ready to leave.

When Gopal pulled into his driveway, it was late afternoon. His head felt oddly still, as it always did when alcohol started wearing off, but Gopal knew that he was drunk enough to do something foolish. He parked and walked down the road to Mrs. Shaw's. He wondered if she would be in. Pale tulips bloomed in a thin, uneven row in front of her house. The sight of them made him hopeful.

Mrs. Shaw opened the door before he could knock. For a moment Gopal did not say anything. She was wearing a denim skirt and a sleeveless white shirt. She smiled at him. Gopal spoke solemnly and from far off. "I love you," he said to her for the first time. "I am sorry I didn't invite you to the fair." He waited a moment for his statement to sink in and for her to respond with a similar endearment. When she did not, he repeated, "I love you."

Then she said, "Thank you," and told him not to worry about the fair. She invited him in. Gopal was confused and flustered by her reticence. He began feeling awkward about his confession. They kissed briefly, and then Gopal went home.

The next night, as they sat together watching TV in his living room, Mrs. Shaw suddenly turned to Gopal and said, "You really do love me, don't you?" Although Gopal had expected the question, he was momentarily disconcerted by it, because it made him wonder what love was and whether he was capable of it. But he did not think that this was the time to quibble over semantics. After being silent long enough to suggest that he was struggling with his vulnerability, Gopal said yes and waited for Mrs. Shaw's response. Again she did not confess her love. She kissed his forehead tenderly. This show of sentiment made Gopal angry, but he said nothing. He was glad, though, when Mrs. Shaw left that night.

The next day Gopal waited for Mrs. Shaw to return home from work. He had decided that the time had come for the next step in their relationship. As soon as he saw her struggle through her doorway, hugging sacks of groceries, Gopal phoned. He stood on the steps to his house, with the extension cord trailing over one shoulder, and looked at her house and at her rusted and exhausted-looking station wagon, which he had begun to associate strongly and warmly with the broad sweep of Mrs. Shaw's life. Gopal nearly said "I missed you" when she picked up the phone, but he became embarrassed and asked, "How was your day?"

"Fine," she said, and Gopal imagined her moving about the kitchen, putting away whatever she had bought, placing the teakettle on the stove, and sorting her mail on the kitchen table. This image of domesticity and independence moved him deeply. "There's a guidance counselor who is dying of cancer," she said, "and his friends are having a party for him, and they put up a sign saying 'RSVP with your money now! Henry can't wait for the

40

party!'" Gopal and Mrs. Shaw laughed.

"Let's do something," he said.

"What?"

Gopal had not thought this part out. He wanted to do something romantic that would last until bedtime, so that he could pressure her to spend the night. "Would you like to have dinner?"

"Sure," she said. Gopal was pleased. He had gone to a liquor store a few days earlier and bought wine, just in case he had an opportunity to get Mrs. Shaw drunk and get her to fall asleep beside him.

Gopal plied Mrs. Shaw with wine as they ate the linguine he had cooked. They sat in the kitchen, but he had turned off the fluorescent lights and lit a candle. By the third glass Gopal was feeling very brave; he placed his hand on her inner thigh.

"My mother and father," Mrs. Shaw said half-way through the meal, pointing at him with her fork and speaking with the deliberateness of the drunk, "convinced me that people are not meant to live together for long periods of time." She was speaking in response to Gopal's hint earlier that only over

41

time and through living together could people get to know each other properly. "If you know someone that well, you are bound to be disappointed."

"Maybe that's because you haven't met the right person," Gopal answered, feeling awkward for saying something that could be considered arrogant when he was trying to appear vulnerable.

"I don't think there is a right person. Not for me. To fall in love I think you need a certain suspension of disbelief, which I don't think I am capable of."

Gopal wondered whether Mrs. Shaw believed what she was saying or was trying not to hurt his feelings by revealing that she couldn't love him. He stopped eating.

Mrs. Shaw stared at him. She put her fork down and said, "I love you. I love how you care for me and how gentle you are."

Gopal smiled. Perhaps, he thought, the first part of her statement had been a preface to a confession that he mattered so much that she was willing to make an exception for him. "I love you too," Gopal said. "I love how funny and smart and honest you are. You are very beautiful." He leaned over slightly to suggest that he wanted to kiss her, but Mrs. Shaw did not respond.

Her face was stiff. "I love you," she said again, and Gopal became nervous. "But I am not in love with you." She stopped and stared at Gopal.

Gopal felt confused. "What's the difference?"

"When you are in love, you never think about yourself, because you love the other person so completely. I've lived too long to think anyone is that perfect." Gopal still didn't understand the distinction, but he was too embarrassed to ask more. It was only fair, a part of him thought, that God would punish him this way for driving away his wife and child. How could anyone love him?

Mrs. Shaw took his hands in hers. "I think we should take a little break from each other, so we don't get confused. Being with you, I'm getting confused too. We should see other people."

"Oh." Gopal's chest hurt despite his understanding of the justice of what was happening.

"I don't want to hide anything. I love you. I truly love you. You are the kindest lover I've ever had."

"Oh."

For a week after this Gopal observed that Mrs. Shaw did not bring another man to her house. He went to the Sunday board meeting of the cultural association, where he regaled the members with jokes from *Reader's Digest*. He taught his first Hindi class to children at the temple. He took his car to be serviced. Gopal did all these things. He ate. He slept. He even made love to Mrs. Shaw once, and until she asked him to leave, he thought everything was all right again.

Then, one night, Gopal was awakened at a little after three by a car pulling out of Mrs. Shaw's driveway. It is just a friend, he thought, standing by his bedroom window and watching the Toyota move down the road. Gopal tried falling asleep again, but he could not, though he was not thinking of anything in particular. His mind was blank, but sleep did not come.

I will not call her, Gopal thought in the morning. And as he was dialing her, he thought he would hang up before all the numbers had been pressed. He heard the receiver being lifted on the other side and Mrs. Shaw saying "Hello." He did not say anything. "Don't do this, Gopal," she said softly. "Don't hurt me."

"Hi," Gopal whispered, wanting very much to hurt her. He leaned his head against the kitchen wall. His face twitched as he whispered, "I'm sorry."

"Don't be that way. I love you. I didn't want to hurt you. That's why I told you."

"I know."

"All right?"

"Yes." They were silent for a long time. Then Gopal hung up. He wondered if she would call back.

For the next few weeks Gopal tried to spend as little time as possible in his house. He read the morning papers in the library, and then had lunch at a diner, and then went back to the library. On Sundays he spent all day at the mall. His anger at Mrs.

Shaw soon disappeared, because he thought that the blame for her leaving lay with him. Gopal continued, however, to avoid home, because he did not want to experience the jealousy that would keep him awake all night. Only if he arrived late enough and tired enough could he fall asleep. In the evening Gopal either went to the temple and helped at the seven o'clock service or visited one of his new acquaintances. But over the weeks he exhausted the kindheartedness of his acquaintances and had a disagreement with one man's wife, and he was forced to return home.

The first few evenings he spent at home Gopal thought he would have to flee his house in despair. He slept awkwardly, waking at the barest rustle outside his window, thinking that a car was pulling out of Mrs. Shaw's driveway. The days were easier than the nights, especially when Mrs. Shaw was away at work. Gopal would sleep a few hours at night and then nap during the day, but this left him exhausted and dizzy. In the afternoon he liked to sit on the steps and read the paper, pausing occasionally to look at her house. He liked the sun sliding up its walls. Sometimes he was sitting outside when she drove home from work. Mrs. Shaw waved to him once or twice, but he did not respond, not because he was angry but because he felt himself become so still at the sight of her that he could neither wave nor smile.

A month and a half after they separated, Gopal still could not sleep at night if he thought there were two cars in Mrs. Shaw's driveway. Once, after a series of sleepless nights, he was up until three watching a dark shape behind Mrs. Shaw's station wagon. He waited by his bedroom window, paralyzed with fear and hope, for a car to pass in front of her house and strike the shape with its headlights. After a long time in which no car went by, Gopal decided to check for himself.

He started across his lawn crouched over and running. The air was warm and smelled of jasmine, and Gopal was so tired he thought he might spill to the ground. After a few steps he stopped and straightened up. The sky was clear, and there were so many stars that Gopal felt as if he were in his village in India. The houses along the street were dark and drawn in on themselves. Even in India, he thought, late at night the houses look like sleeping faces. He remembered how surprised he had been by the pitched roofs of American houses when he had first come here, and how this had made him yearn to return to India, where he could sleep on the roof. He started across the lawn again. Gopal walked slowly, and he felt as if he were crossing a great distance.

The station wagon stood battered and alone, smelling faintly of gasoline and the day's heat. Gopal leaned against its hood. The station wagon was so old that the odometer had gone all the way around. Like me, he thought, and like Helen, too. This is who we are, he thought—dusty, corroded, and dented from our voyages, with our unflagging hearts rattling on inside. We are made who we are by the dust and corrosion and dents and unflagging hearts. Why should we need anything else to fall in love? he wondered. We learn and change and get better. He leaned against the car for a minute or two. Fireflies swung flickering in the breeze. Then he walked home.

Gopal woke early and showered and shaved and made breakfast. He brushed his teeth after eating and felt his cheeks to see whether he should shave again, this time against the grain. At nine he crossed his lawn and rang Mrs. Shaw's doorbell. He had to ring it several times before he heard her footsteps. When she opened the door and saw him, Mrs. Shaw drew back as if she were afraid. Gopal felt sad that she could think he might hurt her. "May I come in?" he asked. She stared at him. He saw mascara stains beneath her eyes and silver strands mingled with her red hair. He thought he had never seen a woman as beautiful or as gallant.